WILD CHRISTMAS

WILD HEART MOUNTAIN: WILD RIDERS MC

BOOK TWELVE

SADIE KING

LET'S BE BESTIES!

A few times a month I send out an email with new releases, special deals and sneak peeks of what I'm working on. If you want to get on the list I'd love to meet you!

When you join you'll get access to all my bonus content which includes a couple of free short and steamy romances plus bonus scenes for selected books.

Sign up here:
authorsadieking.com/bonus-scenes

WILD RIDERS MC

AN INTRODUCTION

Welcome to Wild Heart Mountain home of the Wild Riders MC.

If you love damaged heroes and curvy girl romance, then you'll love the Wild Riders MC.

This group of ex-military bikers fall hard and fall fast when they encounter the curvy women who heal their hearts.

Expect forbidden love, age gap, forced proximity, fake relationships, single dads, single moms and off-limits love with protective heroes who will do anything for the women they love.

Spend some time with Wild Heart Mountain's Wild Riders MC, the MC that's all heart.

Let me introduce you to the members...

Ex-military buddies **Raiden, Quentin and Travis** formed the Wild Riders MC when they got out of the military and wanted to create a place for veterans who love to ride.

They set up their headquarters in a compound on the side of Wild Heart Mountain.

Travis, whose road name is Hops, runs the Wild Taste Bar and Restaurant, and secretly crushes on his best friend's sister.

Quentin, also known as Barrels, runs the award-winning Wild Taste Brewery located out the back of the restaurant. He was a First Class Sargent in the army and you wouldn't want to cross him. Especially where his little sister is concerned…

Colter, or Vintage, is a motorbike mechanic and runs the bike shop. He collects old bikes and loves all things vintage especially the bubbly Danni and her 1950's curves.

Calvin also known as Badge, is the local Sheriff and his uptight views are shaped by loss.

Joseph, or Lone Star is a recluse whose military experiences have given him a distaste for humanity.

Grant goes by Snips. He's the local barber and recently discovered he has a child. He's learning to navigate life as a single dad.

Arlo earns the road name Prince because of his charming and personable nature. He loves getting under the skin of Maggie, the shy pastry chef.

Davis begins the series as a prospect. Younger than most of the other men, he came out of the military with diminished hearing. His hearing aids make him shy with women and he keeps himself hidden away.

Specs would rather read a book than talk to anyone.

Bit Rate is a grumpy single dad widower in need of a nanny.

Judge is a military lawyer and always does the right thing, until he meets the curvy woman who makes him question his world view.

Luke becomes a prospect after Raiden finds him drinking himself to oblivion in a strip joint. A wheelchair user since he lost both his legs in Afghanistan, Luke finds new purpose with the MC, but can he find love?

Marcus goes by Wood because his family own the local sawmill and it's his medium of choice. He channels his PTSD into his art, creating sculptures that attract the attention of an arts journalist from the city.

On the other side of Wild Heart Mountain is a town called Hope and nestled in the hills is the Emerald Heart Resort. During the summer, it's a popular destination for tourists and in winter, they come for the ski season. Perfect for a snowed in romance…

Stay awhile in Wild Heart Mountain and explore the other series set here.

WILD CHRISTMAS

WILD RIDERS MC

A grumpy single dad and a nanny in a feel-good holiday romance.

I don't like Christmas; it's too messy.

But when the new nanny moves in, she fills the house with sunshine and Christmas songs. They make my ears bleed, and she makes my blood run hot.

But Freya's the nanny; she's off-limits and only here until my sister arrives.

But when Freya leaves, I realize too late what she means to me.

Can I convince her I'm not the miserable grump she thinks I am and prove to her that even a Christmas grinch can be happy with the right woman?

Wild Christmas is a single dad and nanny, grumpy/sunshine holiday romance featuring an ex-military biker and the curvy girl he falls hard for.

www.authorsadieking.com

1
FREYA

My foot hits the break and my jaw drops as Mr. Martell's so-called cabin comes into view. I lean forward, peering through the windshield until I can see all three stories of what can only be described as a mansion made of wood.

Mr. Martell told me to meet him at his cabin for the interview and I was expecting something small and cozy nestled in the woods, not the multi-story mansion with a turret poking out on top surrounded by trees on three sides and sitting on a cliff's edge with a view of the valley and the mountains beyond.

A delicious shiver creeps down my spine. It's like something out of a fairytale only made of slatted wood.

Strains of "Last Christmas" blast out of my car speakers as I creep forward and park next to a Tesla, which seems far too white compared to my mud-splattered SUV. No one can keep a car that white in the mountains, and I wonder if he's got a garage full of cars hidden away somewhere and the Tesla is just for show.

I cut the engine, cutting off George Michael, and am plunged into silence broken only by the rustle of the wind from the surrounding trees.

My younger self might have been intimidated by the sight of wealth, but two years working as an au pair in France have numbed me to it. I never saw a place like this in France or in any of the European countries I accompanied the family to on their many vacations though.

There's something about the cabin, despite its size, that's distinctly North Carolinian, and that makes it feel like home.

A late November chill has me pulling my coat tight around my chest as I walk over to the covered entrance. I love this time of year when the weather starts to bite, and I'm smiling as I head over to the huge pillars that hold up the second level balcony and lead to the entrance.

I'm halfway to the door when the roar of an engine coming up the gravel drive gets my attention.

I turn around as a motor bike roars into sight. It's approaching too fast, and gravel kicks up under its wheels. I jump out of the way just in time as it slows down and parks next to my SUV.

The man on the bike is clad in black leather that hugs his taut frame. He pulls the helmet off and runs a hand over his dark hair, smoothing the short cut back into place. A set of thick eyebrows frown at me, and his mouth is set in a scowl that emphasizes his smooth jaw.

"You're early."

The smile slips off my face as it dawns on me that the hottie with the scowl is my potential new employer. As he slides off the bike I'm struck by his size, broad-shouldered and tall, not at all what I expected from a computer geek. He pulls himself up to his full height, which is at least a foot taller than me. But I won't be intimidated by a man wearing a scowl. My time in France taught me that too.

I check my watch, taking my time to respond. "Only by five minutes."

He grunts and unbuckles the saddle bag on the back of his bike. From it he pulls a laptop bag and a backpack and a bunch of cables, surprising me by how much he can fit in there.

He strides over to the door, and I follow even though he hasn't said anything else to me.

Aunt Maxine warned me that Mr. Martell was taciturn, which is a polite way of saying a grumpy ass.

"I'm Freya," I say to his retreating back, figuring it's best I start talking rather than follow him in silence. "My Aunt Maxine said you were in need of a temporary nanny."

He props his knee against the door and rests the laptop bag there while he punches in a code on the key panel. The door unlocks with a click, and he turns the handle, then retrieves his bag. I think about offering to help, but he doesn't seem like the kind of man who accepts help.

"I know who you are," he says. "Judge told me you were turning up."

"Judge?" I wrack my brain trying to think of who Judge might be.

Mr. Martell puts the laptop and cables down on a bench in the hallway and carries the backpack with him down the corridor.

I hesitate on the threshold. He hasn't invited me in, but Aunt Maxine assured me that the interview was set up. I learned boldness from the French too, so without waiting for an invitation, I follow him down the hall.

"Judge is Will's road name, the man your aunt works for," Mr. Martell explains.

Aunt Maxine told me Will was part of a motorcycle club for veterans and that Mr. Martell is in the club too. Which means he's a veteran and has a road name too, probably Grumpy, or Rude, or Nice Ass, because I can't keep my eyes off the way he moves in those tight leathers.

Pulling my gaze away from his perfectly formed butt, I follow Mr. Martell into the kitchen. He dumps his laptop on the marble kitchen island which takes up almost the entire length of the room. Four black wooden stools are tucked in on one side, and beyond is a dinner table and living room set consisting of two enormous couches, with the biggest flat screen TV I've ever seen mounted above a brick fireplace.

The cushions on the couches are neatly in place. There's nothing on the dining room table, and the only ornaments are a couple of matching photo frames in the same black metal as the light fixtures. It looks like a show home, not a home where two little girls live.

I'm beginning to wonder if I've got the right place.

Mr. Martell dumps his backpack on the kitchen island and for the first time looks up at me properly. I stare back at him and fold my arms over my chest.

"You are Mr. Martell, right?"

He frowns. "Yes. And you're Freya, twenty-four years old. You worked as an au pair in France for two years and three months. You have your degree in early childhood education, your background check is current, and you are qualified in children's first aid. You like arts and crafts, music, you learned to ski in the Alps, and you've spent your last two summers on a yacht. You can cook, you like reading, and you've traveled to more countries in Europe than you've been to states in America."

I stare at him as his green eyes bore into mine, wondering how the hell he knows how I spent my summers.

"Not all of that is on my CV."

He shrugs. "I looked you up online."

I take a step back. "Is that legal?"

Mr. Martell looks behind me, completely ignoring the question. "Did you bring your things? I need you to start straight away."

I stare at him, trying to process what's just happened. I think he just offered me the job. But I haven't even had the interview yet.

I don't even know if I want the job. I have a bit of money saved and Aunt Maxine said I can stay with her as long as I want, but I'm keen to get on my own two feet and get settled in somewhere.

But this guy is so arrogant that he assumes I'm falling over myself to work for him.

"I don't know anything about you or your girls. What makes you think I want the job?"

He raises his eyebrows in what I think is an amused expression, but it's hard to tell because he's still scowling.

"Because you're here for an interview. It usually means you want a job."

I open my mouth to protest, but he cuts me off.

"I'm Nate. I work with computers. I have clients all over the mountain, and I'm sometimes called out on short notice and at all hours. If a small business has a computer problem in the middle of the night, they don't want to wait till morning to fix it. I need a live-in nanny so I can be sure there's always someone here for the girls.

"They are six and four. The oldest, Dora, is at school, and Maisie will join her next year. They like arts and crafts and music, which is why you'll be a good fit.

"I emailed your past employer, and she gushed about you. The job is yours. You start today."

I fold my arms in front of my chest. Half of me is impressed that he's done his homework on me, but it would have been nice to have had a chance to tell him about my experience rather than have him digging around the internet without my permission.

The more time I spend with the arrogant but annoyingly hot Nate, the less certain I am I want the job.

"Aren't you part of a motorcycle gang?"

He smirks, and it's annoyingly handsome on him. "A motorcycle club, yes. The Wild Riders. We're all ex-veterans and all our business is legit, if that's what you're worried about. We own the Wild Taste Bar and Restaurant as well as a bike mechanic's shop and an art studio."

An art studio doesn't sound very badass so maybe they aren't all bad, which is what Aunt Maxine told me. But I'm still not sure.

"Why did your last nanny quit?"

He unzips his backpack and pulls out a small bag, and from it he gently pulls out a computer part and lays it on the bench, frowning at the thing.

"She didn't like me."

I bark out a laugh and he looks up at me, his expression serious. Oh, he's not joking.

"The contract is only for six weeks until my sister arrives to take over. You can have Christmas Day off if you want, but I do get called out during holidays, so if you can stay, I'll pay you double."

I must be frowning, because one look at me and he holds up his hands. "Okay, triple."

My eyebrows shoot into my head. This guy must be desperate, and I wonder if I remain silent if he'll keep raising the price.

"You've got an entire suite of rooms at your disposal, a bedroom, separate bathroom, and a living area. Like I said, I need you here in case I have to leave in a hurry, but we're not friends. We're not roommates. You've got your own space, and when you're not with the girls, I expect you to stay in it."

"Wow." My mouth drops open. The arrogance of this man. I was never treated this rudely by any of the wealthiest families I crossed paths with during my time in France. I'm not going to put up with it now.

I open my mouth to tell him I'm not taking the job when the hum of an engine snatches my attention. Through the window, I glimpse a large classic car pulling up out front.

"Is that a Cadillac?" It seems as out of place on the mountain as a Tesla.

"That'll be Danni, dropping the girls off. She's been helping me out while I'm between nannies."

The car door open and two little girls scramble out, their hair wild as they run for the front door. For the first time since I've met Mr. Grumpy Pants, the scowl leaves his face and his expression softens. "They wanted to meet you."

"Oh no…" I start to say, but it's too late.

The door to the cabin bursts open, and two little girls barrel down the hall. They slow to a trot when they see their father, and the youngest crashes into the back of the oldest.

"Are you the new nanny?" the oldest, Dora, asks with wide hopeful eyes as deep green as her father's. I don't have the heart to tell her I'm not taking the job.

"Maybe," I say.

She seems to take that as a yes, because she jumps from one foot to another and the biggest, warmest smile spreads across her face. "I made a clock in school today."

She pulls a clock face out of her school bag and proceeds to tell me how to tell the time. Meanwhile, the youngest has gone to her father, and he scoops her into his arms. She puts her little arms around his neck and plants a kiss on his cheek. Nate smiles, revealing a dimple on each cheek that I had no idea was hiding there.

I'm fascinated by the change that's come over him upon the arrival of his daughters. He kisses the cheek of the little girl and nuzzles into her neck, making her giggle.

Suddenly with the laughter of little girls, the house feels like a home.

A woman in a red polka dot dress with its skirt flaring out and her hair in a 1950's style role waves from the door.

"I can't stop. Bettie's asleep in the back."

"Thanks Danni," Nate calls.

She glances at me with a warm smile. "Sorry I can't stay to meet you properly. I'm sure I'll see you at the club."

I'm not sure what club she's talking about, and the woman frowns at my confusion.

"Make sure you bring her to the club, won't you Bit Rate. Don't keep her locked away here."

She waves goodbye, and I turn to Nate. "Bit Rate?"

"It's my road name. Danni's one of the old ladies at the Wild Riders MC."

I nod slowly, wondering about this man who loves computers and bikes and his girls. There's more to Nate Martell than a tight pair of buns, and that curiosity as much as the little hand that slips into mine makes me decide to take the job.

Dora squeezes me hand, "Can I show you your room?

I made you a card, and you can sleep with Bongus so you don't get scared."

She tugs at my arm, and the last of my doubts leave me. The girls need a nanny, I need a job, and it's only for six weeks. Maybe I can stay out of the way of their grumpy dad, and we can all get along just fine.

This time when she tugs on my hand, I let her lead me out of the room. "Show me where I'll be sleeping."

2

NATE

I slide the graphics card into the back of the PC, and it falls into place with a satisfying click. I pick up the back panel and hold it in place. The tiny screws are delicate, and I take one in my hand.

"Why aren't you working in your office?" I glance up to find Maisie staring up at me, her brown eyes round and curious.

I can't tell her it's because I have an unexplainable need to be in the same room as the new nanny. "Hold this in place while I screw it in."

She climbs onto the dining room chair and kneels so she can reach the panel. Her tongue pokes out in concentration as she holds the panel in place, allowing me to clip one of the tiny screws to my magnetic screwdriver. I turn the screw in place and move onto the next one.

At the other end of the table Freya hunches over colorful cardboard, talking softly to Dora as they glue pieces of fabric onto the card.

"We're making Christmas cards," Maisie informs me.

"Maisie," Dora whines, "it's supposed to be a surprise."

The scowl on her face is as good as any of mine. She looks like she wants to hit her sister, and the last thing I want is for my girls to show their true colors on Freya's second day here.

"I can't see the cards from here. Are you making one for Danni?"

The scowl fades as she scrambles to find a new piece of cardboard.

My girls fight like cats when they get each other going, and I don't want Freya to see that side of them too soon or she night leave. And I desperately don't want her to leave.

From behind the PC I watch her; I've been watching her all day. She's wearing leggings and an oversized sweater that hides the full curvy figure she's got hiding under there. I know, because I saw her in a swimsuit in photos online, her arms crossed over her body shyly, a sarong covering her thighs.

I poured over her photos longer than a prospective employer should have, but they're in the public domain. It made me wonder who else is looking, and that thought angers me. I'll need to speak to her about what she puts online. But if I bring that up now, after only knowing her two days she'll think I'm creepy.

Instead I've been watching her move around my house, confident in the new space, humming Christmas songs although it's only November and tapping her feet when she thinks no one's looking.

From the moment I set eyes on Freya, smiling out of every single photo she's put online, I knew I had to have her here, in my house, bringing that good energy to the girls.

But it's more than that, a nagging voice whispers. I shake the voice out of my head and concentrate on the PC.

Dora finishes up her card and skips off to wash the glue off her hand. I only hope the girls told Freya about the no glitter rule.

Freya stretches, and I try really hard not to notice the way her sweater creeps up her body when she stretches her arms over her head. I finish up what I'm doing and slip the flashlight off my head.

"Do you always work with one of those on?" She smiles at me, and my chest squeezes a little. This woman is beautiful when she smiles.

"Sometimes, when I need to see what I'm doing."

Her smile widens like I've made a joke, only I get the feeling that I am the joke.

Freya puts the finished cards to one side of the table and starts tidying up the crafts.

"Girls, come help tidy up," I call to the girls. They scamper down the hall and come to help without fighting about it which is unusual. They must want Freya to stay as much as I do.

"When do you put your Christmas decorations up?" Freya asks.

"We just have a tree," Dora says mournfully. "A fake one."

Freya pauses as she slides the colorful paper together and looks up at me. "You don't like real trees?"

"They drop too many needles." She frowns at me like I'm weird. "Clogs up the vacuum," I explain.

Freya tilts her head and looks at me curiously as if I'm a museum exhibit. "You like to keep things neat, don't you?"

I shrug. "That's what ten years in the military does to you."

She shakes her head and looks down at the bits of crafts on the table. I can't help it; I like everything in order. Nothing wrong with that.

"Is that why there's no glitter in the craft box?"

She's quick. "Correct. It gets everywhere. There's a glitter ban in this house."

Her eyes go wide in surprise, but she doesn't push the issue.

"So you don't put up any other Christmas decorations? No tinsel, no streamers, no wreath on the door?"

I shake my head. "Nope."

Freya puts her hands on her hips and stares at me. "I love Christmas." She smiles, and her face lights up. "I was thinking I could make some streamers with the girls, hang some tinsel, make a signpost for Santa…"

The girls have gone quiet but Freya bubbles along like a stream, moving around the room no doubt imagining where she'd put all these messy decorations.

"You must have stockings to hang over the fireplace?"

The girls shake their heads and Freya turns on me, and I suddenly feel like the worst dad in the world.

"You don't decorate for Christmas?" She's genuinely stunned, and I feel like the grinch who stole Christmas.

"It's messy," I say lamely.

"You have two little girls; it's supposed to be messy."

The girls look at me carefully, no doubt seeing my defenses waver. "Can we decorate this year, Daddy?" Dora clutches my knee, and her eyes are wide are pleading.

"I'll keep it neat," says Freya quickly. "No glitter, and we'll take it all down afterwards."

"The day after Christmas," I say firmly.

"On the sixth of January, as is tradition," Freya says with her hands on her hips.

She's negotiating with me over Christmas decorations. I like it.

"January first. That's my final offer."

"Fine." She smiles, and I'm glad I'm letting her decorate just to see that smile. The girls jump up and down in excitement and start babbling about every way they're going to turn my neat living area into a winter wonderland.

I've heard enough. I need to drop this PC off with a client, and I'll work at the club for the rest of the afternoon.

I leave them to their planning, but all I can think about is the glimpse I got of Freya's tanned stomach when her sweater rode up and what it would feel like to run my hands over her skin.

3

FREYA

I stack the last of the dishes in the dishwasher, add some dishwashing detergent, and turn it on. Upstairs the sounds of the girls laughing reach my ears, making me smile.

Nate may be a grumpy ass during the day, but he's a softie when it comes to his girls. He insists on doing the bedtime routine with them, bathing them and reading to them. I imagine them now tucked up in bed either side of the big man while he reads them a story.

I leave the pots and pans on the kitchen side. I don't mind doing the washing up. It's not in my job description, but Nate's cooked for me every night so it only seems fair. But after that first night, he asked me not to do the washing up because I didn't do it properly. I've never been critiqued on my washing up before, but if he wants me to leave him the dishes, I'm not going to complain.

I fill the kettle with water and lean against the

counter as I wait for it to boil. It's gone quiet upstairs, and I imagine Nate kissing the girls goodnight and pulling blankets over them.

I pour myself a mug of chamomile tea to take up to my room. But instead of heading up straight away, I linger for a few minutes scrolling through my phone.

Soon I hear Nate padding down the stairs. He comes into the kitchen, and my heart flutters in my chest. His hair is ruffled and his expression soft, as it always is after he's spent time with the girls. He wears a green hoodie that accentuates the color of his eyes and makes it hard to look away.

"Is it okay if I do some baking?"

Nate looks at me like I've grown two heads. "What, tonight?"

"Tomorrow. I thought I could make gingerbread cookies with Maisie and decorate them when Dora gets home from school."

He runs the water in the sink and adds a generous pour of dish soap.

"Of course. Why do you think I wouldn't let you bake?"

"Um. Because baking is messy."

He pauses and turns to face me. "You're not going to get flour everywhere, are you?"

I jut my chin out. "Probably. That's what happens when a four year old helps."

He frowns, and I continue before he changes his mind. "But what also happens is she learns to measure things, to stir, and has fun licking the bowl."

17

He turns back to the dishes. "Fine. But you might need to pick up some ingredients."

"I'll check what you have."

I pull up my favorite gingerbread recipe on my phone and proceed to check the cupboards for what he has. As expected, the cupboards are in perfect order and everything I pull out is within the use by date. I bet he checks his cupboard regularly and throws out anything that's exactly past the date.

I make a list on my phone of what I'll need to get from the store tomorrow.

Meanwhile Nate has finished up the dishes and leaves them drying on the rack.

He puts the kettle on and pours decaf coffee beans into his grinder. "You want something?"

"No thanks. I've already got a tea." I wonder if this is the night when he'll put on the big TV in the living room and invite me to watch something with him. I wonder what he's into. Sci-fi and action films would be my guess.

But once he's made his coffee, Nate picks up his mug. "Goodnight."

He heads out the door and to the back of the cabin where his offices and workshop are.

"Goodnight," I call after him wondering what he does all evening. Perhaps it's work, but the guy's got to rest sometime.

Every night I've been here, the house goes quiet once the girls are in bed. I have no idea where Nate goes at night. Feeling bold, I creep down the hall in my socks until I'm outside the door to his office. But there's no noise coming from inside.

Another mystery involving the taciturn man.

Quietly, I retrieve my chamomile tea from the kitchen and head upstairs.

I shouldn't complain. When he said I had a suite of rooms, he wasn't joking. The room opens to a cozy living area with plush carpet that my feet sink into and thick curtains. There's a loveseat and an armchair that folds out so I can rest my feet.

A TV is propped on one wall and a bookshelf on the other with a collection of frayed paperbacks that previous nannies must have left behind.

Through the living area is a room leading to my bedroom with a private bathroom attached, complete with spa bath and a large window looking straight into the woods.

I set the tea on the coffee table next to Bongus, the stuffed blue elephant that Dora leant me, and head to the bookshelf. I've finished one book already, and I peruse the shelves and select a book with a suave-looking man with a bare muscular chest on the cover. The book promises to make me swoon, and I sit on the couch and pull a blanket over me and settle in for the night.

4

FREYA

"It's fine," I tell Aunty Maxine a few days later. "The girls are great. Dora doesn't stop talking and Maisie is so sweet. She just wants to give me hugs all the time."

I turn the heater up in my car while I give my aunt a rundown on my first few days on the job, talking about the girls and not mentioning their hot grumpy dad.

"We're decorating tomorrow. I've just been to the shops to get everything."

"He's letting you decorate? I heard Nate was a Christmas Grinch." She sounds skeptical, and I'm immediately defensive of Nate although I'm not sure why.

"He's not that bad. A little strict, but he probably has his reasons."

"Hmm," she mutters, not convinced. "You can come back anytime, you know, if it gets too intense. It's not right that you're stuck up in that room all on your own like a prisoner."

I'm regretting telling my aunt about the arrangements and spending every night alone in my room.

"It's fine, really. I'm getting a lot of reading done."

Which is an understatement. I've read almost every book that was left on the shelf, and today when I was in Hope I joined the local library and checked a stack of books out. I've never had so much time to myself.

In France the family didn't include me every night, but they didn't not include me every night either. I watched movies with the family, helped cook meals, and played backgammon with Martine, the mom. And I had evenings off where I met up with other au pairs and went to the English cinema and sat in cafes drinking strong French coffee and eating way too many pastries.

It was fun, but there was always something going on. It was always busy. I craved the nights when I stayed in, reading the books I found in the English bookshop.

Not everyone would understand this, but I like the solitude. I like evenings tucked up and reading quietly. At least for a few nights I do. By now, it's getting a little lonely.

I wonder what Nate does in the evenings. I don't even need to hang out with him. Just to be in the same room as him would be nice, me reading my book and him doing whatever it is he does.

I stifle a sigh so as not to worry Aunt Maxine.

"Have you heard from your mom?" she asks.

I think of the patchy video call we finally had yesterday, because she couldn't connect on Thanksgiving when I was with Aunt Maxine. There were blue skies and flax sun umbrellas behind her, and she kept cutting out because internet is patchy on the small remote island in the Pacific where she's staying.

"She's fine. Drinking cocktails in the sun and waiting for Dad to arrive."

Dad's off for three weeks' vacation, and they decided to spend a hot Christmas together in the Pacific rather than a cold one in the mountains. The island is close to where Dad is based, and with their 25th wedding anniversary this year, they wanted to do something special.

I was invited of course, but pristine beaches and endless sun have lost their allure after two years in the south of France with a family with their own private yacht.

And they'd never say it, but it's their special anniversary, and I'm sure they want to spend it just the two of them. My parents get precious little time together since Dad was deployed to the Pacific.

"Are you sure you want to work over Christmas?" Aunt Maxine asks me for the hundredth time. "There's always room for you at Karl's."

My aunt is spending Christmas with my cousin and his family. I know I'd be welcome, but this job is so short and he's paying me triple to work over the holiday, so I don't mind staying. Besides, I spent Thanksgiving with Aunt Maxine and her other son came up for a few days, so I've had some good family time.

"I don't mind working, really. I'm needed here, and it's triple pay. It's too good to turn down."

I end the call to my aunt and turn the engine off. I step out of the car, and the cold hits me. It's the last day of November, and the air temperature has dropped especially this high in the mountains. Everyone's predicting snow before Christmas.

I breathe in deeply, loving the feeling of cool air in my lungs.

This is why I came back. Because sun and sand suit some people but give me winter in the mountains any day and I'm happy.

I'm more comfortable in snuggly layers before a roaring fire than in a swimsuit at the beach. The French family couldn't understand it. They thought I was mad to want to come back here. But I guess I'm a mountain girl at heart.

I grab the shopping bags out of the back and head into the house. Tomorrow is December first, which means it's the day we're decorating for Christmas.

It's also a Sunday, so both the girls will be around to help. I just wonder if their grumpy dad will join us.

The girls are watching a Christmas movie when I come in. It's the first time I've seen the big TV on. I dump the bags in the living room and then wonder if that will be a problem with Mr. Clean.

"Where's your dad?" I ask the girls, and Dora mumbles something and points down the hallway to the side that leads to the laundry and garage.

I head in that direction and find him in the garage, his motorbike propped up on its side with parts strewn on the floor and a tool case open next to him. Nate sits on the garage floor watching something on his phone. He's laughing as he watches and I lean on the door, not wanting to interrupt.

He's handsome when he smiles. The lines of his face disappear, and the dimples creep into his cheeks. He looks younger, carefree. This must be what Nate looked like before he had two little girls to raise on his own.

He notices me at the door and glances up. His smile widens when he sees me, and my stomach flutters at the way he lights up.

"This guy's hilarious."

I walk over, taking it as an invitation to join him. I crouch next to Nate and look at the phone he's holding. He scrolls back a bit and plays the video again.

A man holds a part to a Harley, the same model as what Nate has. As he talks about the importance of not getting too much grease on the part, a toddler appears in the background. The kid waves to the camera, then pulls a funny face. The man has no idea the kid is there and keeps talking while the kid continues to smile and wave at the camera.

Soon the kid is joined by what I assume is his younger sister. She crawls into the garage behind the man and stares at the camera with a baffled expression on her face. Finally the guy realizes there's a show going on behind him and turns to his kids. They laugh and scamper away while their dad tries to catch them.

It's funny, and I laugh alongside Nate while the man in the video calmly gets back to his instructional video.

"I like this guy, Josh." Nate pauses the video. "His kids are always getting in the way. It's funny. It's real."

He shows me another snippet of a video where the boy keeps running through the video pushing a firetruck while Josh does his best to keep going. Nate's doubled up laughing, and I guess it's relatable from one dad to another.

Nate sets his phone down so it's leaning against the toolbox and picks up the part that looks similar to what Josh, the guy in the video, was holding.

He frowns at the part and inserts it under the engine of his bike. "I think that's where it goes."

"Don't you have a bike shop at your motorcycle club headquarters?"

"Yup." Nate twists the part, frowns some more, and pulls it out and looks at it. "Give me any laptop, computer, or electronic and I'll fix that for you. But don't ask me to do DIY, and don't ask me to fix your car."

"Why don't you take it to the shop?"

He wipes his hands on a greasy rag. "I can't admit to the guys I can't fix my own bike. If it needs serious repairs, I'll take it in. But a tune up I should be able to do myself."

Sounds like man logic to me, but I don't say anything.

"Besides, I've got Josh." He indicates his phone. "Aside from being entertaining, he's incredibly informative. I've learned everything I need to know about bike mechanics from this guy."

He gets up off the floor, and I stand up too. Our arms

brush as we stand up together, and a bolt of heat shoots through me. I gasp and grip my arm, wondering if he felt it too. But when I glance up at him his expression is neutral, and when he speaks, he's lost the friendliness from a few moments ago. "Did you want to see me about something?"

I crash back down to earth. It's a reminder that we definitely aren't friends. He's my employer, and sharing a laugh over a YouTube video isn't going to change that.

"I picked up some supplies for decorating tomorrow." He look confused. "You know, for Christmas."

He frowns. "Is it the first of December tomorrow?"

I hope he's not going to change this mind; the girls will be gutted if he does. "We're making streamers, and there is definitely no glitter or cotton wool." I rattle on before he can stop me. "Do you want to join us for the decorating?"

He runs the rag over a grease spot on his hand, frowning at it when it doesn't rub off.

"No. I said I'd stop by the club tomorrow and check the servers. They need an update, and Sunday is a good time to do it."

"Okay." I try not to let the disappointment show in my voice.

"I'm just going to leave the supplies in the lounge for the night, if that's okay?"

"Sure." A ghost of a smile plays across his lips. "I like things clean, but I'm not a tyrant, Freya."

The way he says my names makes a shiver dance down my spine. His fingers brush my shoulder, and my breathing quickens.

"You've got a hair…"

I glance up, and Nate's staring at me intensely. His gaze darts to my lips, and I know without a doubt he wants to kiss me.

"Can we watch it again?" Dora comes bounding into the garage followed by her little sister. I turn toward the door as Nate turns away.

"You can watch one more movie, but not that same one. Pick something different."

"Will you watch too, Daddy?" she asks mournfully. "Please…"

Nate glances at his bike still in pieces and sighs. "Yes, I'll watch. Just give me ten minutes." The girls squeal in delight and Maisie barrels into him, hugging his knees. He laughs, and once again I'm taken aback by the change in him when his girls are around.

Dora tugs on my arms. "Can you watch too, Freya?"

"Please…" begs Maisie, extracting herself from her dad and turning her wide brown eyes on me.

I glance at Nate but he's gone back to the bike, putting the pieces back together. My heart thunders in my chest. If the girls hadn't interrupted, I'm sure we would have kissed. But Nate's crouching on the floor, frowning at his bike as if nothing happened.

He's not looking at me, not giving any indication if I'm welcome to join them or if I should retreat to my room.

I turn back to the girls and their smiling hopeful faces. I don't want to say no.

"Sure." I match Dora's enthusiasm. "You got popcorn?"

5

NATE

"How's the new nanny?" Snips pulls out the chair opposite me, spins it around, and straddles it.

So many ways to answer him flit through my mind. She's got perfect curves, her smile makes me smile, and I'm having indecent thoughts of the kind I haven't had in years.

"She's great with the girls," is all I say. "They really like her."

"Good." He sounds as relieved as I am. "Maybe this one will stick around."

A memory of Freya from yesterday tucked up on the couch and laughing at *Elf*, her cheeks rosy from the heat of the fireplace, pops into my mind. "I hope she sticks around too."

I must have put too much warmth into my voice, because Snips raises his eyebrows at me but wisely doesn't say anything.

"Have you thought of doing DNA testing for the girls?"

His words hit me like a punch to the gut, and I sit up straight in my chair. "Why would I do that?"

He pulls a foil packet out of his pocket. "Me and April have done it and Bailey too. They analyze your genes and tell you if you're susceptible to any diseases so you can take preventative measures. Turns out both me and Bailey have the gene for macular degeneration. It doesn't mean we'll necessarily get it, but if we eat more carrots now and get regular eyes tests, we can limit our chances."

He waves the packet around in his hand. "I thought you'd be into all that science shit, so I got you a testing kit."

He puts the kit on the table, and I eye it warily.

He's not wrong. The idea of analyzing your genetic makeup fascinates me. But I'm more concerned about what else it might reveal.

"It was a two for one offer, so it was free anyway. Thought you'd be the most into it."

I scratch my jaw as I listen to Snips tell me all about the test results and what insights it's given him and April about Bailey.

There's always something new in parenting, and I start to wonder if I'm doing it wrong if I don't get a DNA analysis of my girls. Hell, there's a hell of a lot I'm doing wrong, having indecent thoughts about the nanny being the top one.

Snips heads out the back, and I pack up my laptop. I've hidden at the clubhouse for most of the day, and it's time to get home and see what the hell she's done to my house.

I go out via the workshop. We're not officially open on a Sunday, but Luke has the garage door up and is tinkering with his wheels. He got the road name Chariot, and that's the perfect word to describe his wheelchair adapted bike.

There's a side platform that he rolls up before lifting himself onto the bike. The brakes and accelerator are operated by hand. But what's most impressive is the paint job. Bright flames lick the side of the setup, making it look like a Roman chariot of the Gods.

My bike sits in the corner, plain by comparison. "How's she looking?"

"We'll need to work on her tomorrow, and I'll get her back to you in a day or two. Just needs an oil change and a tune up. You could probably have done that yourself."

I nod at the younger man. "The thing is I don't know shit about bikes."

He raises his eyebrows. "I guess I don't know shit about computers."

"Correct. So you fix my bike, and next time your laptop needs an update, you bring it to me and I'll sort you out."

Luke grins and indicates his chariot. "You need a lift home?"

"Thought you'd never ask."

He wheels himself onto the platform and folds his seat against it. I take a seat on the passenger side. I'm not used to riding pillion, but the kid is excited to tell me all about the bike and I can't deny him the pleasure.

He's as passionate about bike mechanics as I am about fixing tech. I don't understand all the bike terms he's telling me, but I understand the passion and enthusiasm.

He's a different kid than the one who turned up two years ago broken and feeling sorry for himself. He lost both his legs in Afghanistan, which is a shitty thing for anyone and especially a guy so young.

It's good to see him happy now as he tells me about every adaptation he's made for his bike.

We chat for a while, then he starts her up and we head home. I'll bring the Tesla back tomorrow and tow my bike home, but right now I need to see what the hell Freya's done to my house.

6

NATE

*B*efore I open the door, I hear them singing. It's some famous Christmas shit that gets blasted every year whenever you go into a grocery store or any shop, even at the damn gas station.

I turn around, wondering if I should go back to the clubhouse, but Luke is already retreating down the drive. There's nothing for it but to go into the cabin.

I punch in the code and push the door open. Alongside the music and way too loud bass, the sounds of laughter reach my ears.

I pad down the hallway and pause when I get to the living room. The blinds are drawn, and in the middle of the room is Dora's speaker shooting multicolored laser lights onto the white walls.

Hanging from the rafters are colorful streamers made out of pieces of crepe paper woven together. They should look scraggly and forlorn, but in the flashing lights they seem cheerful, and knowing that my girls made them gives them a festive rather than messy look.

The fake tree sits in the corner wrapped in tinsel so tight it's as if it's been done up in bubble wrap and ready to ship.

Green tinsel is draped over the fireplace, which I'll have to remove because that is clearly a fire hazard.

They haven't seen me yet, and I lean against the door frame and watch them.

Freya has her back to me and her head is tilted back as she belts out the lyrics to what is fast becoming my favorite Christmas song. The girls sing along with her, Dora shouting the words and Maisie trying to keep up, laughing when she doesn't know the words.

Maisie jumps on the spot, waving her arms about, which is her four-year-old best dance move, while Dora twirls and swirls, catching Freya's hand in hers as Freya spins her around.

My chest tightens as I watch them. This is what a happy home looks like. This is what a woman brings to a home, fun and laughter and chaos.

Is this what the girls would have had if their mother had lived? I shake the thought out of my head. There's no point in thinking about what might have been.

If their mother had lived, she would have taken them from me in the divorce settlement. I would have been restricted to only seeing my girls on weekends when I was on home leave, because I would probably still be in the military. The thought makes me shudder. Of course I would have preferred for Becky to have lived. No one would wish what happened on their worst enemy, let alone the mother of their children. But nonetheless, I'm grateful for how my life has turned out and that I get to see my girls every day.

The last nanny was nothing like Freya. When I told Freya she left because she didn't like me, that was only half true. The girls didn't like her. She was strict and made them cry. I'm strict and I make my girls cry sometimes when I tell them off, but that's a father's prerogative. There certainly wasn't any dancing and singing and jumping about the living room, with mesmerizing hips swaying the way Freya's do.

The song changes and Freya spins around. She stops mid spin when she sees me. Her eyes go wide in the most adorable way. Her skin is flushed, her cheeks rosy, and her hair hangs loose and whips around her face. She lunges for the speaker and hits stop. The music continues coming out of her phone, a tinny sound, and she grabs that and turns it off too.

"Sorry, I didn't hear you come in."

She looks anxious, and she must think I'm a real ogre if she's scared of playing a bit of music.

"It's fine." I switch on the lamp by the door so I can fully assess what they've done to my living room.

Dora runs up to me. "Do you like it, Daddy? We made streamers and we hung tinsel. And we did the tree."

Maisie scampers up to me and raises her arms, wanting to be picked up. She's always been clingy, but I don't mind. I scoop her up in my arms and bury my face in her neck, making her giggle as I kiss her.

"Which ones did you do, MayMay?" She twists in my arms, wanting to be put down. Then she tugs on my shirt and leads me over to a piece of cardboard that's by the Christmas tree.

Shapes are scribbled on the cardboard, and she points to it proudly. "A sign for Santa."

I pick the cardboard up and nod at it seriously while she tells me all about the blobs of color which are reindeer that she's drawn. In Dora's childish scrawl is written: 'Santa stop here.'

Freya comes over and crouches next to me. She bites her lower lip, an anxious look on her face. "Is this okay? Is it too much?" She gestures around the living room. "The girls made some reindeer they want to put on the wall, but I didn't know whether it was okay to use sticky tack on your walls."

I've allowed sticky tack in the girls' room to put their pictures up, but I don't want it ruining the walls in the rest of the house. But when I look around at their happy faces, I wonder if I've been too strict. Walls can be painted over, but my girls will only be young once. "I've got some in my office. You can put some up, just not around the fireplace."

The girls squeal with delight, and Dora runs off to get the sticky tack.

Maisie tugs at my hand, and I looked down at her wide eyes. "Can you dance with us, Daddy?"

"I don't dance, sweetie."

Her face falls, but I haven't danced since I was an adolescent at the school dances. Dancing isn't my thing.

Her bottom lip wobbles but my brave girl doesn't cry, even though her un-fun dad has disappointed her once again. "But you can put the music back on if you want to keep dancing. I'll watch as I make dinner."

Freya puts the music back on, this time turned down a few notches, and I head to the kitchen.

Dora comes back with the sticky tack, and soon my pristine white walls are decorated with kid's Christmas art and more streamers.

The three of them start dancing again, and I do my dinner prep on the counter facing out so I can watch them.

But it's not my girls I'm watching. It's Freya. The way she moves to the music, the carefree way she sings along to the songs, her easy laugh, and the adoring way my girls look up at her.

This is what this cabin needs.

The thought hits me like a blow to the chest. I'm a grumpy bastard, I know that. I like things neat and clean and orderly. Freya brings fun and laughter and chaos. She makes the house into a home.

A few hours later the girls are tucked into bed after dinner, and I come into the kitchen to finish the washing up. Freya is in the living room crouched over a box and packing unused craft bits into it.

She stands up when she sees me. "Where do you keep the vacuum? I'll run it around to get the tinsel."

"The robovac will get it when it does its nightly

rounds." I indicate the robotic vacuum cleaner tucked under a side table.

"Okay." She nods. "I've never seen one of those in action."

"I'll show you."

I flick it on, and the robovac shoots out of its holding casing. It heads straight for Freya, and she jumps out of the way. In her hastiness she bumps into me, and I grab her elbow to steady her.

Her gaze flicks to mine, and her eyes go even wider. "It startled me."

I should let her go, but I don't. I hold onto her longer than necessary, because she feels too damn good. There's a piece of green tinsel caught in her hair, and I brush it away with my fingers.

"Tinsel." I hold it up and release her elbow. She steps back and carefully away from where the robovac's running over the carpet.

My heart thunders in my chest. Having her this close makes my palms sweat, and I'm sure she must hear my heartbeat.

I'm rooted to the spot as she bends down to retrieve the craft box from the carpet and out of the way of the robovac.

"Thanks for today." Freya plops the box of craft supplies on the table.

I pull myself together, ignoring the way she makes my pulse race. "The girls loved it. They like you."

She smiles. "It's what most people do, Nate, decorate the house for Christmas."

She's teasing me, and I rub my chin where growth from the day has left a blunt stubble. "Yeah, I know."

She puts the kettle on and makes a mug of the chamomile tea she likes. "You want a decaf?"

It's been less than a week and Freya knows my routine. "Thanks." She knows I'll make a decaf coffee and disappear to my gaming room, where I'll play online with a bunch of guys I've never met until I crawl to bed sometime after midnight.

But tonight I don't feel the draw to the game like I usually do. Tonight I don't want Freya to leave with her chamomile tea and disappear upstairs.

"Goodnight." She takes her mug like she does every night and turns for the door.

"Do you want to watch a movie?" I blurt out.

Freya turns slowly, looking confused. "Together?"

My eyes dart to her lips, and I lick mine. "Yeah."

She shrugs. "Okay."

7

FREYA

*N*ate chooses *Die Hard* proclaiming it to be a Christmas movie. By the time it finishes, we're spread out on opposite ends of the sofa.

He makes himself another decaf and hands me another chamomile tea. I'm not ready to go to bed yet, and I guess he isn't either.

"Tell me about France. It must have been nice to travel."

The tea is too hot, and I place it on the coffee table. "It was nice to see different places and the family was great…"

He raises his eyebrows at me. "But…?"

"But I missed the mountains."

"You missed home."

I shake my head, because that isn't quite it. "I'm not sure where home is. My father is in the navy, and we traveled around a lot when I was young."

He nods slowly, taking in what I'm saying.

"My mom…" I trail off, not wanting to speak ill of my mother. I don't like to discuss her mental health problems, but Nate feels like someone I can open up to. "My mom found it hard to cope on her own."

A frown crosses Nate's face. "It's hard, being a military wife." There's a bitterness to his tone that makes me glance up at him, but he's staring straight ahead into the fire. "Not everyone is suited to it."

I sit back on the cushions and run my finger over the edge of one, playing with the tassel. "Mom was put in a facility for a while. To recover, is what I've been told. I was sent to live with my Aunt Maxine."

"Your aunt who lives in Hope?"

"Yeah. She's great." My mood lifts, thinking of Aunt Maxine. "I've got three cousins, all grown up now, and when you've been an only child, it's great coming into that environment. I loved it. I didn't understand at the time what was going on with Mom, and I was used to Dad not being around and moving about, so it just seemed like one more stop on the road."

I pull at the cushion, remembering the two years spent at Maxine's place in the town of Hope on the side of the mountain. The summers were spent swimming in the lakes, hiking the trails, playing hide and seek in the backyard, and other invented games with my cousins.

The way Aunt Maxine would dance around the living room with all of us trailing behind her. She taught me how to laugh in the face of whatever life threw at you, and I've been dancing ever since.

"It's the only place that ever really felt like home."

Nate nods thoughtfully and takes a sip of his drink. "So you're going to stay here now? No going back to France?"

There's an edge to his voice and I frown, wondering why he cares so much. His sister's coming to take over the nanny position, so I won't have a job in a few weeks.

I think about the email I got this morning from Martine, my old employer in France. The new au pair hasn't worked out as she hoped, and she's begging me to come back after Christmas. She offered a generous pay increase if I accepted. "Maybe."

Nate stiffens. "You're leaving Wild Heart Mountain?"

He seems concerned, and my heart gives a little flutter, which is stupid. He's probably just thinking about what happens if it doesn't work out with his sister. "I'm not sure. I might go back to France."

"You got a boyfriend there?" His voice is harsh, and I glance at him. He's staring at me intently, and for a crazy moment I wonder if he's jealous. But that can't be right. Nate is at least ten years older than me; he hates chaos and messiness, and that's what I am.

"No." He relaxes into the pillows. "No boyfriend."

"Good," he mutters, and my pulse quickens. I'm inexperienced with men, but I'm sure there's a vibe here.

Which is bad. I can't be crushing on my boss.

As we've been talking we've gravitated toward the center of the couch, and my thigh bumps into his. His hand is resting on his knee, and his pinky creeps out and caresses my thigh. A shimmer of heat courses up my body and makes me tingle between the legs.

Oh, this isn't good. Nanny rule 101: Don't get involved with the dad. But as I look into his intense eyes, I wonder if it's too late. He's leaning into me and I catch his scent of coffee and pine cleaning spray, which is oddly attractive on him.

My heart rate kicks up a notch, and this is really bad. I can't kiss the hot single dad.

I lean forward, breaking the physical contact, and snatch up a photo of the girls that's on the coffee table.

That was too close, and I can't get distracted again. If I get involved with my employer, I'll never get another job.

It's something Aunt Maxine warned me about, and her words ring in my ears. "When you're living under a man's roof he will see you as his property, particularly a young pretty girl like you. Don't get involved. No matter what they promise you. Remember, you're also living with their wife. And the wife must always be respected."

My French family was never like that. Frank, the dad, treated me like a daughter. But this situation is different. Nate makes my stomach flutter every time he's near in a way I've never felt before. And Nate doesn't have a wife.

I study the photo more carefully than I need to, trying to clear the thoughts from my head.

Dora has Nate's dark hair and intense eyes and the same frown as her father. "She looks a lot like you."

I dare a look at Nate and he's sitting back on the couch sipping his coffee, as unruffled as if the thigh caress never happened. Maybe I imagined it. Maybe his finger bumped me accidentally rather than caressed me.

I stare intently at the photo again. It looks recent judging by the look of the girls. While Dora has her dad's features, Maisie has light hair, brown eyes, a round face, and an easy smile.

"Maisie doesn't look like you at all. Does she take after her mother?" I glance back at Nate, and he's sitting stiff on the couch with a scowl on his face.

"She takes after her mother, looks wise." He stands up abruptly and takes his mug to the kitchen. "Turn the lights off on your way out."

I gape after his retreating figure as he heads down the hall and to his office.

I thought we'd made progress spending an evening together, but Nate has closed himself off. I regret bringing up the girls' mother. I heard she died in a car accident when Maisie was only a few weeks old. He must still be torn up with grief over her.

8

NATE

The next few weeks pass in a blur. I get used to the smell of cinnamon from all the baking Freya's doing. The Christmas songs don't seem so bad now, and I hum along as I get to know the lyrics to her favorite.

The girls spend hours playing in the living room, rearranging the decorations on the Christmas tree and making more and more streamers. They fight less, both caught up in the excitement of Christmas.

Freya hums as she moves about the house, and I find myself smiling every time she comes into the room.

We watch another movie together and then another, making our way through Freya's favorite Christmas movies. But I stay firmly on the far side of the couch, not wanting to throw myself at Freya again even though it's taking everything I have not to.

I keep to my office in the evenings when we're not watching a movie, not trusting myself to be around her.

Since I nearly kissed her on the couch, I've kept my distance even though it's killing me. But she's the nanny, and I can't take advantage of that even if she did want me.

I regret storming off that night the way I did.

She can't have known the fear her words sparked in me, and I'm not ready to voice them.

I apologized the next day and ever since I've kept myself guarded, maintaining a distance and keeping it professional.

It's the day before Christmas Eve, and Maisie is at forest school today. Even with a nanny, I like to get her out with other kids a few times a week to socialize. Maybe she'll learn the people skills I seem to lack.

The house is quiet without the girls, and I stay in my office transferring data off a client's PC while I get in a few games of *Tour of Duty*.

My character darts behind an abandoned shed, but I don't see the enemy on the other side. I fire, but it's too late. Red splatters the screen, and my character grunts as the bullet wound to the chest ends him.

"Shit."

I pull off my headphones and throw them down on the desk. I can't concentrate on shooting bad guys knowing that Freya is wandering around the house on her own.

It's her day off and I thought she'd head out of the house, but the imminent snowstorm has kept her inside. I hate to think of her sitting up in her room alone.

It never bothered me with the last nanny, but Freya is

different. Freya has soft curves and a smile that lights up the room.

I shake the thought out of my head. She's too young for me, too innocent.

I check the download from the client's files and head to the kitchen to get some lunch. I expect to run into her at any turn, but the house is quiet.

Once in the kitchen, I grab some bread and leftover chicken and a few other bits and pieces from the fridge to make a chicken sandwich.

There's a lot of food, and I don't know if Freya's had lunch yet. It would be nice to sit and eat with her. To hear more about her life, her dreams, and find out what she's going to do in a few weeks when Sydney, my sister, turns up.

I have my misgivings about my sister being a nanny. But I'm not going to turn her away when she needs a place to stay and a job. Besides, Maisie will be starting school in March, so it's only a few months until all she has to do is collect them from school when I can't.

The thought of my little girl heading off to school makes me heart squeeze. How did my baby girl get so big so fast? Needing to see something of my little girl, I head to her room.

It's decorated in rainbow colors with animal decal on the walls. Her snuggly toys are arranged on the bed, and I imagine her talking to them this morning in the way she does before kissing them goodbye.

I pick up her favorite, Hoppity, a mangy rabbit with half its ear missing. It's been through the wash several times, but the damn things keep hanging on. Not that I'd never throw it away. She's had Hoppity since she was a baby. They gave it to her in the hospital after the accident, and she's clung to it ever since.

Hoppity smells like Maisie, like glue sticks and crayons from the crafting she loves doing. I breathe in the scent, missing my little girl even though I only saw her at breakfast a few hours ago.

I put Hoppity back on the bed nestled between a fluffy elephant and a bright blue teddy bear. Her pajamas are on the floor even though I've told her a hundred times to pick them up. I fold then neatly and put them on the end of the bed.

Her craft box is open on the floor and felts scatter the area. I pick those up and straighten a few other things in her room.

There's an adjoining door to Dora's room and I head in there, hoping my oldest has got the hang of tidying up after her.

I stop short when I see Freya sitting on the bed. She's got a photo album open on her lap, and she closes it quickly when she sees me.

"Sorry. Dora had it out this morning, and I was just tidying it up." Her eyes dart to the side, and she looks guilty.

"It's okay." I hold my hand out for the photo album. "The girls like to look through it often."

She hands me the album, and I sit next to her on the bed. It's a small single also crowded with stuffed animals, so that when I sit next to Freya our thighs bump up against each other.

An electric shock courses through my veins, and my dick twitches to life. Which is entirely inappropriate considering where we are, but I can't control the effect this woman has on me.

I open the photo album and am greeted with the chubby face of baby Dora, which never ceases to make me smile.

"She was an adorable baby," coos Freya.

"She was," I agree. "I missed her birth. I was deployed, and she came early. By the time I came back, she was already two weeks old."

Becky lies on the hospital bed, her eyes dark with exhaustion and a wan smile on her face as she holds Dora up for the camera.

There are a lot of pictures of Becky with her new baby. I want the girls to remember their mom. The photos were taken by my ex-mother-in-law who flew in from Texas to be with her daughter and never quite forgave me for not being at the birth of her first grandchild.

I flip the page to the first pictures of me with my daughter, my face unlined and my eyes wide with wonder. I can't believe it was only six years ago. I look like a much younger man.

Then me again in my military uniform kissing a two month old Dora before heading off for another deployment.

The time was always too short with my family. Dora

wouldn't remember me when I got back, and by the time she got used to me again it was time to go.

There are more pictures of Dora and her mom, Becky looking better in a floaty summer dress, Dora on her hip, a chubby one year old now. Becky's hair is loose, and her flawless skin shiny and bright. She looks so young, too young.

I turn another page, and there are more photos of me and Dora and Dora and Becky. There are none of the three of us together, and I wonder if Freya notices.

"Do you miss her?" Freya's voice is a whisper, and I know she's asking about Becky.

I think about the fight we had the last time I saw her. How her face that I once thought pretty was screwed up in resentment. How she yelled at me and called me all the names under the sun even though I was the one who should have been angry.

I remember the girls crying in the house, Maisie's newborn mewls and Dora's toddler howls. How I begged her to calm down and not scare the girls, to come inside and talk in the morning.

"I miss the girls having a mom," I say. "I'm sorry for what happened to Becky, but we were getting a divorce."

"Oh," Freya says her shock evident. "I'm sorry."

"Don't be. Becky wasn't suited to life as a military wife. She was too young when we married."

Freya doesn't say anything, and her silence relaxes me. I feel like I can open up to her. "She cheated on me."

Freya gasps, and when I glance at her she looks horrified. A single tear rolls down her cheek, and my chest squeezes that this woman feels so much. "I'm so sorry that happened to you."

My thumb brushes the tear away. "Are these tears for me?"

She nods and my thumb lingers on her cheek, tracing the curve of her cheekbone. "You feel too much."

Her warm breath brushes my cheek, and I close the distance between us with my lips, pressing my lips against hers. She's soft and warm and tastes of the strawberries she had on her cereal this morning.

Freya moans, and I pull away. She looks up at me with round, innocent eyes, and I'm reminded of how young she is. Too young. Too young and innocent, and I'm not going to repeat the same mistakes I made with Becky.

"Sorry." I stand up abruptly, and the photo album slides off my lap and onto the floor. I reach to pick it up at the same time as Freya, and our foreheads bump together.

"Sorry," we say at the same time.

She rubs her head and I rub mine, and I'm as awkward as I always have been around a beautiful woman, like the geeky guy who won all the math competitions at school and never the girl.

I was the guy who spent his lunch breaks in the computer room while the cool kids played football or softball or any of those other games I've never seen the skill for.

I was a mathlete, which is way less cool than being an

athlete when you're in high school and stupid stuff like being cool matters.

It was at a career day when I was recruited into the army. The man in the neat military uniform said they could use someone with my skills.

I joined the Signals and never looked back. I liked the routine of military life; it was neat and orderly until the accident and the honorable discharge I took to raise my girls. Becky's mom wanted to take them back to Texas, and for once she encouraged me to stay in the military. But I wasn't giving up my girls. I gave up the army instead.

I moved back home to raise them in the mountains and took on client work that mostly only uses a fraction of my skills. But occasionally the government calls, and I help on special projects when they need my specialist skills.

But day to day I'm updating laptops and switching PCs off and on again for elderly clients who look bemused when they sit in front of a screen.

It's worth it for my girls.

My instinct is to make a hasty retreat from Freya and what just happened. But I'm not that awkward teenager anymore. I'm a grown ass man with enough experience to know what I'm feeling for Freya is different. So I take a deep breath, put my fears behind me, and say what I came here to say.

"Do you want a chicken sandwich?" She smiles shyly, and its's disarming, and I don't think I conveyed to her what I really want. "I mean, do you want to join me for lunch? Do you want to have lunch with me?"

9

FREYA

*A*s I follow Nate to the kitchen for lunch, I press my fingertips to my lips. They tingle from where he kissed me, and my entire body feels more alive than it ever has. He pulled away from the kiss, but I wanted him to keep going.

I want to find out where that kiss would lead. I thought he was going to retreat like he so often does and I walk quietly behind him, certain he's going to change his mind about lunch.

When we get to the kitchen the food's already pulled out of the fridge, and he lays four slices of bread on the counter and starts buttering them.

He started to open up about his wife, and I have so many questions. It's a revelation that they were separating and I feel for him, the man away protecting his country while his wife carried on behind his back. It must have felt like a huge betrayal.

There's a PC on the table, which I've come to see as a

recurring theme. Even though Nate has an office and workshop, he says the light is better out here. I think he likes to be in the family area when the girls are around so he can be near them.

His backpack is on the table with computer parts spewing out of it. My gaze catches on a silver foil packet with the name of a DNA testing company written across it.

I pick up the package. "I've heard about these; you can trace your ancestry and find out loads of stuff that's in your genes."

Nate glances at the packet and frowns. "Snips gave it to me. I'm not sure if I'm going to do it."

I turn the packet over in my hands. "I think it would be interesting to see where you came from. It might be surprising."

Nate takes the packet off me and shoves it deep in his backpack. "Maybe." He walks back around to the where he's making the sandwiches. "You want mayo or mustard?"

His tone has a finality about it, and I take it the subject is closed. "Mayo please."

Nate squeezes mayo onto my sandwich, puts a slice on top, and puts it on a plate. He slides it across to me, and I take a seat on one of the stools.

The sandwich is good, and we eat in silence for a few moments.

"Have you always been into computers?"

He swallows his bite of sandwich and nods. "I was the kid who spent recess in the computer room. Teachers used to come to me to get their laptops fixed. I made a bit of money on the side doing it."

"It's impressive. I don't know a thing about tech."

He shrugs. "Not really, not once you learn how. Just most people don't bother to learn."

He's being modest. I'm pretty sure most people wouldn't know how to do what he does. I finish my sandwich and take the plate to the sink. I don't want to go back to my room yet. I want to hear more about Nate.

He's gone quiet since he opened up to me earlier, and I worry I've made him sad by bringing up old wounds. "It's not your fault, you know."

"What isn't?"

"That your wife cheated. I didn't know her, obviously, but that seems like a shitty thing to do to someone when they were off defending your country."

He shakes his head. "It was a long time ago. I should never have married her. She was too young, too much of a free spirit. She's not the type of woman who could be left alone."

"She must have known what she was getting into, marrying into the military."

He drops his plate into the dishwasher and leans against the counter next to me.

"I was a bad husband, Freya. I shouldn't have left her alone with the kids. But she told me she was fine."

I think about my own mom and the struggles she had with me.

"How did you find out she cheated?"

"She told me." Something passes across his face, and I regret bringing it up.

Nate takes a deep breath and runs a hand through his hair. When he speaks, it's so quiet I have to lean in to hear him. "I'm not sure that Maisie's mine."

He looks the saddest I've ever seen him, and I clutch the side of the bench as a wave of emotion hits me. "No..."

He looks up at me with tortured eyes. "The night before the accident, we had an argument. I had found out about the cheating a few weeks before and thought we could have an amiable split. But she got angry at me and said Maisie wasn't mine. I stormed out of the house and went to stay with Judge for the night. It was the next day she had the accident. Went off the road coming down the mountain. She was killed instantly. The girls were in the car without a scratch on them.

"The trunk was packed with her bags. Becky was leaving, to go to her lover or to her mom's I'll never know."

I take his hand, feeling the sadness rolling off him. He loves Maisie. To live this entire time wondering if she's his or not must be torture.

"Oh Nate, I'm so sorry."

He squeezes my hand. "I chose not to believe her. Becky could sometimes say things in the heat of the moment, and those girls needed someone. I try not to think about it, tell myself it doesn't matter..." He shakes his head. "Then Snips gives me this DNA test and I think well, maybe I should find out for sure. Then I'll know one way or the other."

He's torn, I can see it in his face, and I regret bringing it all up.

"Sorry, I brought it up. I didn't mean to pry." I'm just curious about what makes this man tick, about who he is. I want to know every aspect of him.

"Don't be sorry, Freya. I like that you're curious about me." He turns to me, and I realize how close he is. "It gives me hope that maybe you feel like I do."

My breath hitches at his words, and my heart races. "How do you feel?"

His thumb brushes my lip, and he pulls it down. "Like I want to kiss you again."

My skin pimples at his touch, and dampness floods my panties. Everything in me is aching to kiss him, but my aunt's words echo around my head. "Never get involved with the dad. Ever."

But my body wins out. Nate kisses me, and this time I'm ready for him. I meet his lips hungrily, opening up for him.

His hands tangle in my hair and our bodies bump together, sending heat to every place that connects with him.

My hand slides around his neck, and a moan escapes my lips. It feels so right. It can't be wrong, can it?

Then Nate's hands are on me, running over my waist and circling me in his arms, drawing me to him. I banish any doubts from my mind and let the kiss take me.

"Freya," he whispers, "I've wanted you since I saw your pictures online."

His words whispered against my neck send fresh heart sizzling down my veins. His hand slides under my thigh and I lift my leg, hooking it around his waist.

He caresses the tops of my thighs and moves around between my legs. Even through my leggings, the sensation of his hand caressing my pussy makes me gasp.

Nate tilts his head back, and his eyes are deep pools of desire. He keeps them on mine as he slides a hand under the waistband of my leggings. His fingers find my slick folds, and I tremble under his touch.

"You're wet for me, Freya."

The way he says my name sends a new shock of bliss through me. I tilt my head back, and he kisses my neck. His hand moves with precision and sensitivity, stroking my most sensitive areas.

I shouldn't be doing this, but it feels so right and I'm not sure I could stop now. The sensation builds to a peak, and I grip his shoulders as a wave of pure bliss crashes over me.

The sudden sensation makes me cry out and I bear down on him, pressing his palm to me. Before my climax stops he moves against me again, teasing out another orgasm.

This time as I come his finger slides into me. Nate grunts. "You're so fucking tight, Freya."

I grip his shoulder as I shudder through my release. "I haven't done this before, Nate."

He pulls back to look at me, shock written all over his face. "You're a virgin?"

I nod before I realize my mistake. Nate pauses, and my pussy pulses on his palm as the last orgasm winds down.

"Is that a problem?" Nate shakes his head, but his hand slides out of my leggings and he carefully places my leg down by my side so my foot hits the floor.

"I'm sorry, Freya. I got carried away. I forgot how young you are. I shouldn't have started something."

"I'm twenty-four, Nate. I'm a big girl who can make her own big decisions."

I glare at him as anger flares inside me. I was about to give myself to this man, and it seems all he was after was a quick fumble.

"That's not what I meant…"

But I don't stick around to hear what he meant. Tears sting my eyes, and I'm not going to let him see me cry. Aunt Maxine was right. I never should have let the dad kiss me.

10

NATE

Freya runs out of the kitchen before I can explain. She thinks I regret touching her, but that's not it. I regret not taking her upstairs to my bedroom, not laying her down on a bed of fucking roses like she deserves.

I was going to take her virginity in the kitchen, probably bent over the kitchen counter. My dick twitches painfully as an image of a naked Freya bent over my kitchen island pops into my mind.

Fuck. I'm as useless with women as I always have been. Always saying the wrong thing.

I should have grabbed her to me. Told her I haven't stopped thinking about her since she walked into my cabin with her easy smile and love of Christmas songs.

Instead I've made her feel cheap and made her cry.

"Good one, fuck nuts," I mutter to myself.

But this is easily fixed. I'll go upstairs and tell her how

I feel. Tell her that I want to take her out properly, to treat her right like she deserves.

I'm about to head up to Freya's room and hope she forgives me when my phone rings.

It's the daycare where Maisie is, and my heart jumps into my throat when I see the number.

"What happened?" I bark into the phone.

"Oh," comes the startled reply. "Is that Nate Martell?"

I grit my teeth, needing to know my baby girl is okay. "Is Maisie okay?"

"She's fine." The voice is firm but calm, and I relax a little. But only a little, because something must have happened for the daycare to be calling.

"Maisie's got a fever. She's at a hundred point two. Nothing to be alarmed about, but our policy is to send them home if it goes over a hundred."

It's just a fever and not one of the hundreds of scenarios that have flashed through my mind in the last ten seconds.

I sag against the counter in relief. I remember the first time Maisie got a fever and how panicked I was, searching online parenting groups, bundling a sleeping Dora into the car to rush them both to the medical center in Hope.

The nurses were sympathetic to a new widower trying to figure it all out with his kids. I was given a handbook on childhood illnesses and sent home.

Now I know better than to rush to the emergency room whenever one of them so much as coughs. But I still don't take any chances.

"I'll come get her."

I snatch my keys off the counter and head out to the car. If she's okay, I'll stop by the store on the way home and buy something to make it up to Freya, flowers or chocolates or some shit. I dismiss the idea immediately as too cliche. I'll stop by the bookshop instead. I've seen the library books she's always got her nose buried in. I'll grab her a couple of books as well as the roses and chocolates. Better to cover all bases. Then I'll explain to her how I feel.

She might reject me, she might be too young, and she might want to go back to France, but I've got to try.

But first I need to get my baby girl and make sure this fever is nothing to worry about.

I slide into the Tesla and head off, hoping like hell Freya doesn't hate me too much before I get a chance to come back.

11

FREYA

*M*y body's still throbbing as I hear the door close downstairs. I peer out at the dark snow clouds hanging above the valley and see the Tesla's taillights heading down the driveway. A dull ache forms in my chest.

I was ready to give myself to Nate, and he's driven away. What was I thinking?

I was told never to get involved with the dads, and worse never to catch feelings for them. And stupid naive me has gone and done both.

I'm so angry at myself. I could have sworn Nate felt something towards me, but the way he's gone and left me says otherwise.

I sit by the window for a long time until the clouds thicken and snow begins to fall. It's only another week until this job ends. If I could leave now, I would. But it wouldn't be right to leave those little girls alone so close to Christmas.

I'll have to swallow my embarrassment that I naively thought this was something more when all Nate wanted was a bit of fun.

I can get through my remaining time here by focusing on the girls and sticking to my room as much as I can.

I'm watching the snow fall when a car I don't recognize comes up the driveway. It parks in the empty space where the Tesla usually sits and a woman gets out.

She retrieves a suitcase from the trunk and darts towards the house. A moment later the doorbell rings.

Knowing that Nate is out I head downstairs, wondering who the visitor is. I open the door to find a short woman who's all curves. Snowflakes catch on her dark hair, and she peers at me with the same green eyes as Nate.

"You must be Freya, the nanny." The woman smiles, and she's got the same dimples as Nate too. "I'm Sydney, Nate's sister."

Sydney bustles into the cabin, dumping her bag in the hallway, removing her knee high leather boots, and hanging up her winter coat like only family can.

"Nate's gone out." I'm surprised by how steady I manage to keep my voice and hope she doesn't notice my red eyes. "He wasn't expecting you for another week."

"I'm early." Sydney moves through to the kitchen and flicks on the coffee machine. "You want one?"

I shake my head. I don't want to be down here when Nate comes home.

"I was supposed to work over Christmas but the job

fell through, so I thought I'd surprise Nate and the girls and come back early."

She grinds beans, sending the aroma of coffee wafting into the air.

"You're staying here?" I ask.

She frowns at me. "Of course. It means you don't have to work over Christmas either." She misinterprets my look. "Don't worry, Nate will still pay you. But if you want to go to your family, you can now that I'm here."

She grabs a mug from the cupboard, at home in his kitchen. "My brother doesn't think of things like that. He's never been great with people. He thinks everyone likes to work as hard as he does."

She's giving me a way out, and I should be happy. This is what I wanted, to leave. But my heart also sinks at the thought.

"But the girls?" I squeak, not sure I can leave them.

"I haven't seen them in person for a year. I'm dying to spend some time with them. Make sure they're not picking up my brother's gaming habits." She shakes her head. "He was the same as a boy. Spent all his time in his room gaming."

She presses buttons on the coffee machine and it whirs to life, spewing out dark liquid into a mug.

"He does have the best coffee though. One thing about being a complete nerd. When Nate is interested in something, he gets really interested in it."

She takes a sip of coffee and sighs contentedly. "These are the best beans, ethically sourced from Ghana and kept in the freezer. Nate, being Nate, has a self-correcting temperature gage to keep the freezer at the correct temperature for the beans. That's my brother for you. There's not much outside of tech that takes his interest, but when it does, he's all in."

I turn away so she doesn't see the tears that sting my eyes. I thought I might have that attention trained on me. But I was a naive fool.

I'm not sticking around to be embarrassed any longer. Now that Sydney's here, there's no reason for me to stay.

"I'm going to head up and clear out the guest rooms for you."

She shakes her head. "I didn't mean you should leave right now, not if you don't want to. There are plenty of spare rooms. I don't need the penthouse."

She says it with a smile, and I realize I like Nate's sister. The way she speaks about him, you can tell there's a lot of love between the siblings. It wouldn't be right for me to stay now anyway. He's got his family here for Christmas. I'd only get in the way.

I've got my key to Aunt Maxine's. She's away with her son and it will be a quiet Christmas on my own, but it's more preferable than staying here.

It doesn't take me long to pack my suitcase. I put the books back on the bookshelf and throw the ones I borrowed from the library into my bag. I guess that's what I'll be doing on Christmas Day, reading on my own.

Reading is usually what I do for comfort, but the thought makes me feel hollow.

I peer out the window, but the Tesla isn't back.

A layer of white dust covers the ground, and I need to leave now before the snow gets any heavier and the roads gets slippery.

I lug my suitcase downstairs and find Sydney sitting on the couch with her stockinged feet propped up on the coffee table and a magazine open on her lap. An open bag of corn chips is next to her, and a trail of crumbs is sprinkled on the floor and sofa. I wonder if Nate will tell her off for the crumbs and feel a dull ache thinking about it.

"I like what you did to the place." She indicates the decorations. "I assume that was you, because my brother wouldn't think to do something like this with the girls."

"Yeah." I don't trust myself to say anything more, and I swallow hard thinking of the girls and how much I'll miss them. Maybe after Christmas once I've gotten over my embarrassment, I'll pop by to say goodbye to them. It's a downside of the job, getting attached to your charges.

"I'm going to go before the roads get bad."

Sydney nods. "I'm sure you want to get back to your family. I'll let Nate know."

"Thank you." My voice wobbles at the thought of leaving Nate, and for the first time Sydney looks up sharply from the magazine and peers at me with the same frown as her brother.

She stands up, dropping crumbs to the floor that I'm sure her brother will have something to say about.

Her brow furrows, and she takes a step closer to me. "What did that dumbass do to you?"

She says it kindly, but I can't speak because I don't want to break down in front of a stranger. I swallow the tears and put on a fake smile.

"Nothing. I'm just missing my family is all."

She nods slowly like she doesn't believe me. But I'm already heading for the door. "Have a good Christmas."

"You too," she says softly.

I let myself out and get my bags into the car. I don't look back as I drive into the snow, and only once I'm onto the mountain road and heading to Aunt Maxine's do I let the tears fall.

12

NATE

Maisie is lethargic when I pick her up. We stop by the drug store to stock up on kids medicine. I head across the road, carrying Maisie to the local bookstore, but it's closed for Christmas.

It will have to be flowers and chocolates. When I get to the counter of the local store, Larry's wearing a Christmas hat and his nose is red like he's already on the brandy.

"Is Santa coming to visit?" he asks Maisie, but she turns her head into my chest and burrows into my neck.

"Better get home before the snow gets any heavier. You don't want to be out, especially in that toy car of yours."

He chuckles like I haven't heard that joke a hundred times. A Tesla isn't the usual car for the mountains, but it's safe for the kids and electric is the future. I have my bike when I want to joy ride.

Maisie lifts her head to beg me for some candy, and

I'm so happy to hear her little voice that I get her one, and one for her sister too.

I swing past to get Dora from school. It's a little early, but I want to get them home and off these roads before the snow gets heavy.

By the time we get to the cabin, the snow's falling fast. I squint at the car parked in front of my charging post, not recognizing it. It's not until I'm parked and out of the car that I realize Freya's car is gone. A sinking feeling gnaws at my stomach, and I'm suddenly desperate to get the girls inside.

Sydney greets me at the door, throwing her arms around the girls and snatching them into a big hug. Seeing her aunt revives Maisie and she laughs and giggles, reassuring me somewhat.

"Where's Freya?" I ask.

Sydney narrows her eyes at me in a look I know only too well. "She left."

My stomach bottoms out. "You mean left left or left to go to the store?"

"Freya left?" Dora's bottom lip wobbles. "Why did she leave Dad? We were going to have a Christmas dance party tonight."

I give Sydney a look, because sometimes you have to put a spin on things for my kids. "We can still have a dance party."

"No we can't." Dora stamps her foot, and her bottom lip juts out. "You don't dance. Freya dances. Freya's fun. You're not fun, Dad."

She storms off to her room and Maisie follows her,

turning to give me a death stare, so I guess she's feeling better. Now I've managed to drive the nanny away and piss off my kids.

Sydney's looking at me with an amused expression on her face.

"When you say she left, did she…?"

"She had her suitcase with her. I told her she could go now that I'm here. I said you'd pay her, but I'm sure she wants to get home to her family."

I run a hand through my hair. Her family is here, here with me. But I never got a chance to tell her that.

"I have to go." I have to tell Freya how I feel before she thinks I'm some asshole who took advantage of her. But Maisie has a fever and Dora's cross with me.

"I'll take care of the girls." Sydney reads my mind like any good sibling.

"Maisie has a fever, but I don't think it's serious. I gave her a dose of Tylenol. She won't need any more for another four hours, but I'll be back by then." I hope I'll be back with Freya.

I run a hand through my hair, thinking of anything else my girls might need.

"There's stuff for dinner in the fridge. I was going to do tacos but use whatever you want."

Sydney holds her hands up. "Nate, I'll be fine."

I grab the keys to the bike, because the thick tires are better in the snow. In my backpack I stuff the chocolates, and as I stuff the roses in, the petals come off.

"Shit." I'm fucking this up already, and I haven't even got there. Broken flowers aren't going to cut it.

I couldn't get Freya any books, but there's something else she loves. I grab the last things I need and head out the door.

"Go get her!" Sydney calls after me.

13

FREYA

*T*he words dance on the page, but I can't concentrate enough for them to stick in my head. I pull the woolen blanket around me and pull the heater closer to the armchair. Aunt Maxine wasn't expecting me to come back here while she was away, and there's no wood for the wood burner. I should go out and get some from the woodshed, but it's snowing now and I can't find the energy to move.

Instead I close the book and stare at my hands as thoughts of Nate tumble through my head. My chest aches, and I didn't realize how deeply I'd fallen for him and his two little girls.

It will be better to get away from here, to go back to France and forget about the geeky mountain man biker who I should never have kissed.

Music blares out in the quiet street, and I jerk my head up to the window. Someone's playing Mariah Carey, and usually it's my favorite Christmas song but I don't want to hear it right now. Wrapping the blanket around my shoulders, I pad over to the window and peek through the blinds.

The snow's coming down in a steady flutter, and something flashes in the snow. I wipe condensation from the window and peer out.

Laser lights dance on the snow-covered ground, coming from a familiar-looking speaker on Aunt Maxine's front yard. A huge bike just like Nate's is parked out front. My heart leaps into my throat.

"Nate?" I scramble to the front door and pull it open just as the beat kick in. That's when I see him.

Nate's in his biking leathers and Wild Riders MC jacket. A Santa hat sits at a jaunty angle on his head, and he's got his hand over his heart as he sings along to Mariah Carey.

I bark out a laugh, because this is so far from the serious head-in-a-computer Nate that I've come to know.

"What are you doing?" I take a few steps down to the yard, and he sashays over to meet me. He actually sashays with his hips swinging and arms in the air.

"Dance with me, Freya." He offers a hand out to me.

"What is this?"

"It's me apologizing for being an ass. You ran off before I could explain how I feel."

I can barely speak, and my chest feels tight. I don't dare to hope. "And how do you feel?"

He beckons with his hand. "Mariah explains it better than me."

As the chorus kicks in, I take his hand. Nate spins me across the yard, and he moves surprisingly well for someone who claims not to dance.

He pulls me toward him and grasps me around the waist.

"I've been in love with you ever since I saw your pictures online. That might sound creepy. I told myself that was creepy and tried to ignore my feelings. But then you arrived at my house and you smile all the time and you make me laugh and you make me want to goddamn dance. I tried not to love you, Freya, but it's damn impossible. You make me want to laugh, you make me want to smile, you make me want to dance every day for the rest of my life if that's what it takes to have you by my side.

"I'm not good with people, but with you, I'm a better version of myself. You make me want to be the kind of man who dances in the snow at Christmas."

We've stopped moving now, and I stare up at his earnest hopeful face.

"Please say you'll come back. Not as the nanny but as my life partner. I love you, Freya, and I want you in my life always."

His words are everything I didn't know I needed to hear. My heart melts and my breathing steadies. This is where my home is. On the mountain with Nate and the two girls I've come to love as much as their father.

"Yes," I say. "I want that too, Nate. I want to be with you and the girls."

Relief crosses his face and he smiles, making his dimples dance in his cheeks.

"I'm sorry I brought up everything with the girls earlier. You know you're the only father Maisie will ever know."

He steps back and reaches for this backpack that's leaning against his bike. "I've been thinking about that too."

He grabs the foil package with the DNA test out of it. "It doesn't matter if I supplied half the DNA or not. Maisie is mine, and I don't need a test to prove it."

He crushes the package in his hands and something inside snaps. "I was worried for ages that some asshole might turn up to try to claim her. But let him come. I've got four years of caring for my baby girl that proves I'm her dad. I don't give a shit if some fucking DNA says otherwise." He saunters to the trashcan by the side of the house and chucks the test in. "Maisie is mine as much as Dora is, as much as any of the kids we're gonna have are."

My eyes go wide in surprise as a tingling feeling spreads inside me. "You want more kids?"

He crinkles up his nose. "They're messy and unpredictable and no good for my white walls." His hand slides around my waist, and he draws me to him. "But they're also surprising and sweet and the most wondrous pieces of tech I've ever come across. If you want to fill my cabin with kids, I'm all for it." His words, whispered against my neck, spark a delicious tug deep in my belly. "Maybe we should start straight away."

He pulls back to look at me, and his eye are hooded. "If that's what you want."

He kisses me, softly at first as I surrender to his lips

SADIE KING

on mine, then more urgent as warmth spreads through us against the biting cold of the snow.

Then his hands are on my waist and on my hips and the kiss becomes urgent and needy. He steps me backwards until we're pressed against the side of the house. There's a line of trees down the side of the house and where we are is in shadow, masking us from the streetlight and the lights of the laser light speaker.

Nate presses his body to mine and his hardness bumps up against me. I wiggle against him, and he groans my name.

"Freya, careful what you're doing to me."

I run a hand over his chest and to the bulge in his jeans, kneading it with my palm. My fingers work on the zipper, and he stops my hand.

"Your first time should be on a bed with roses. It should be perfect."

"Nate, we're in a snowstorm with Christmas music playing. This is beyond perfect. It's better than I could ever imagine."

He pulls back to study my face. "Are you sure?"

"Yes." I nod. "I'm with you. It's perfect and I'm sure."

His hands continue their exploration of my thighs, sliding up until he hooks under my leggings. He pulls them down, and the cold air hits my bare ass. I grit my teeth in a hiss.

"That's cold."

He puts his meaty hands on my butt, and there's instant warmth. "Let me heat you."

Warmth spreads through my body as Nate's hands

run over my bare skin. He pulls my leggings and panties off my feet, nudging off the house shoes I came out in. When my foot hits the ground it's cold and I wince, but Nate lifts me up.

He leans me against the house and I grip his forearms, strong and muscular under his jacket.

I tug at his zipper and his cock pops out into my palm.

I gasp at the size of him, sticking straight out with a bead of pre-cum catching in the light.

"I don't know if I'll…"

But my words are cut off as Nate tilts my hips so the tip of his cock slides through my slick folds.

"You'll fit, Freya. You were made for me."

He balances me on the end of his dick, nudging at my slick entrance. "I love you, Freya."

I glance up, and he's looking at me with hooded eyes. "I love you too."

Nate slides into me and everything shifts. I grasp his shoulders and cry out, my moans lost in the Christmas music still blaring from the speakers.

He pushes through my virgin barrier and I feel the squeeze, a searing pain for an instant. Then it's gone, replaced by the oddest sensation of being filled up, completely stuffed with the man I love.

"Are you okay?" His voice is choked, and I realize how much he's straining to keep it together. The knowledge gives me power, that this man is about to lose control inside of me.

I rock my hips and Nate groans.

"Careful, Freya," he hisses. "You feel too good."

Chilly snowflakes fall on my bare skin, doing nothing to cool my overheated body. Nate rocks me against the wall, levering my hips to go deeper. I cling to him as my body reaches a higher level of pleasure than I've ever known.

"Nate…" I whine as the pressure becomes too much, "I'm going to…"

My words are cut off as the climax crashes over me. I cling to him, wailing his name as wave after wave of bliss rolls over me.

My back hits the wall and he tilts my hips, going deeper and making me cry out some more. This time when I peak he peaks with me and we climax together, pleasure coursing through my veins at the feeling not only of my own pleasure, but his as well.

"I love you, Freya." He kisses me gently as he lowers me to the ground.

"Can we go home now?" I ask. Because finally I feel like I have a home. Wherever I am with Nate will be my home.

"Of course. Get your things. I'm taking you home."

EPILOGUE

NATE

Christmas Day

Maisie nestles into my chest, her small arms tight around my neck. How she's still awake I don't know. There are beds for the kids made up in one of the rooms upstairs, but despite the big day and the late hour, they're all still awake. Dora is with Rose and some of the other kids playing with her new Barbie doll, Science Barbie. They don't have a tech start-up barbie, so it was the best I could find. The computer coding device for kids is discarded, left at home, not deemed a must show at the clubhouse.

I have one hand around Maisie and the other firmly holds Freya's hand under the table. Since she came back to the cabin with me, I haven't let her out of my sight.

This is the first time she's come with me to the clubhouse, and it's one hell of an introduction. The Christmas Day dinner always is.

The remains of Maggie's latest dessert creation sit on the table. It tasted so good that I had seconds, and now my stomach is so full I can't move. Luckily I don't want to.

Davis made a round of coffees and Raiden poured brandy into mine, and now the adults sit comfortably around the table while the kids are off playing.

I was anxious about introducing Freya to the club, but I needn't have worried. She has way better social skills than me.

On her other side is Specs, and they've been talking all night about books. I had to give him a warning to keep his hands off her when she went to the bathroom, but Specs just shook his head, bemused. The guy knows nothing about love.

Even so, the sooner I put a ring on Freya's finger the better. I want the whole world to know she's mine.

We spent Christmas morning with the girls tearing into their presents. With Sydney and Freya there, Christmas has never felt so fun.

In the afternoon we came to the clubhouse, and it's been absolute chaos with all the kids, old ladies, and anyone else with nowhere to go for Christmas.

I glance at Sydney to check in on how she's getting on. It's been a few years since she last set foot in the club-house, and as we walked in I saw the strain on her face as the memories must have flooded her.

But now she's laughing with Dani and Maggie, and

even Isabella, Prez's queenly old lady, has a smile on her face.

Next to Maggie is Isla, a young woman who I haven't met before. She nurses a baby and keeps her head down so her hair falls half over her face, keeping it in shadow.

Maggie introduced her as the sister of a friend from her pastry school days. No more needed to be said. When a woman turns up looking as furtive as she does and clasping a baby to her chest, we're not going to turn her away. We have the women's refuge center that Lone Star's old lady opened but sometimes it gets too full, so Isla is staying at the clubhouse.

Across the table, Luke keeps glancing at her. He hasn't been able to take his eyes off Isla since she turned up with Maggie. He sat opposite her at dinner and was attentive, passing her the potatoes before she even asked, but as far as I can see he hasn't spoken a word to her yet.

But I see the way his eyes track her every movement. Isla gets up now and paces with the baby to the bar and back. The baby cries, and she jiggles it in her arms. A muslin cloth is flung over her shoulder, and as she walks it drops to the ground. Quick as the lightning painted on the side of his wheels, Luke pushes off from the table and almost runs over one of Danni's kids in his eagerness to get to the cloth.

He holds it up to Isla, and she looks at him properly for the first time. The first smile I've seen since she tuned up here crosses her face. They exchange some words I can't hear, and she takes the cloth and turns away.

Luke watches her like a lost puppy. Poor guy's got it bad.

"What are you grinning about?" Freya squeezes my hand.

"Just watching Luke." Freya follows my gaze. "Seems we're not the only ones falling in love."

I maneuver the now sleeping Maisie to my other arm so I can pull Freya closer to me. "You ready to go home yet?"

She leans closer and nibbles on my earlobe, sending a wave of longing straight to my dick. "I'm ready to be alone with you."

I push the chair back abruptly, startling Maisie awake. "Dora, time to go."

My oldest whines as I knew she would, and it takes some cajoling and a lot of goodbyes, but finally I have everyone in the car and heading home

Sydney lets out a long sigh, and I wonder if the night was harder on her than she let on.

"Can you put the kids to bed?" I ask her when we get in the house. She barely has time to answer before I'm dragging Freya upstairs. Since our first time together we've made love in the shower, against the wall, and finally in the bed. I'll never get tired exploring her body or hearing her laughter.

Freya's the best Christmas present my family needed.

* * *

GET YOUR FREE BOOKS

Sign up to the Sadie King mailing list and get access to all the bonus content including bonus scenes and five FREE steamy short ebook romances!

You'll be the first to hear about new releases, exclusive offers, bonus content and all my news. You can even email me back. I love chatting with my readers!

To claim your free books visit:
authorsadieking.com/bonus-scenes

If you're already a subscriber check your last email for the link that will take you straight to the bonus content.

Wild Heart Mountain

Military Heroes

Kobe brings together a group of military veterans who live on the side of Wild Heart Mountain. Can these wounded warriors find love or do their scars cut too deep?

Wild Riders MC

This group of ex-military bikers fall hard and fall fast when they encounter the curvy women who heal their hearts.

Mountain Heroes

Steamy stories featuring the men and women from Wild Heart Mountain's Search and Rescue and Fire service.

Sunset Coast

Underground Crows MC

Short and steamy MC romance stories of obsessed men and curvy girls.

Sunset Security

A security firm run by ex-military men who become obsessed with their curvy girls.

Filthy Rich Love

Bad boy billionaires of the Sunset Coast and young innocent curvy woman.

His Christmas Obsession

A Christmas romance about an obsessed biker who rides across the country in the snow to reach Cleo before he's even met her.

Men of the Sea

Super short and steamy tales from Temptation Bay of bad boys and curvy girls.

Love and Obsession

A bad boy trilogy featuring a thief, a henchman and an ex-military hitman who finds redemption with his curvy girl.

For a full list of Sadie King's books check out her website

www.authorsadieking.com

ABOUT THE AUTHOR

Sadie King is a USA Today Best Selling Author of contemporary romance novellas.

She lives in New Zealand with her ex-military husband and raucous young son.

When she's not writing she loves catching waves with her son, running along the beach, and drinking good wine with a book in hand.

Keep in touch when you sign up for her newsletter. You'll snag yourself a free short romance and access to all the bonus content!

authorsadieking.com/bonus-scenes

Printed in Great Britain
by Amazon